There is no frigate like a book
To take us lands away,
Nor any coursers like a page
Of prancing poetry ...

Emily Dickinson (1830–1886)
(extract from 'Readers and Riders')

A CIP catalogue record for this book is available from the British Library.

© 1990 A & C Black (Publishers) Ltd

Published by A & C Black (Publishers) Ltd
35 Bedford Row, London WC1R 4JH

ISBN 0–7136–3320–4

Filmset by August Filmsetting, Haydock, St Helens
Printed in Great Britain by St Edmundsbury Press,
Bury St Edmunds, Suffolk

Ink-slinger

Poems about putting words on paper

Edited by Morag Styles and Helen Cook

Illustrated by Caroline Holden

A & C Black · London

The first thing to do in a house
Is find the poet's pen,
Then feed God's mouse
And water Mary's hen.

Anna Wickham

'But it isn't Easy,' said Pooh to himself . . .
'Because Poetry and Hums aren't things you get,
they're things which get you. And all you can
do is to go where they can find you.'
He waited hopefully . . . .

A. A. Milne
(extract from 'The House at Pooh Corner')

Shallow Poem

I've thought of a poem.
I carry it carefully,
nervously, in my head,
like a saucer of milk;
in case I should spill some lines
before I can put it down.

Gerda Mayer

Empty Head

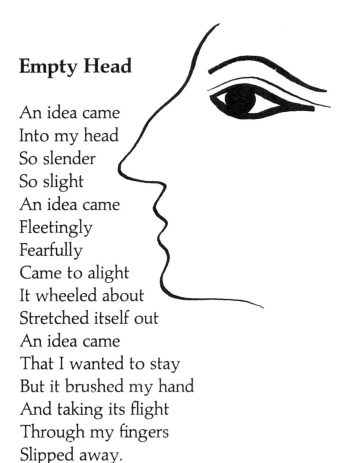

An idea came
Into my head
So slender
So slight
An idea came
Fleetingly
Fearfully
Came to alight
It wheeled about
Stretched itself out
An idea came
That I wanted to stay
But it brushed my hand
And taking its flight
Through my fingers
Slipped away.

Malick Fall

Poetry (or Cricket)

Writing poetry is like fielding
at cricket. You stand on the grass
watching, ready to act.
If you're in the right place
at the right time and looking
in the right direction
you can hope to contribute,
occasionally, something useful
to the game.

And there's always a hope of glory;
a moment may offer itself when everything
conspires in your favour —
the light, the wind, the batsman
(whoever he may be).
A beautifully lobbed ball
will seem to slow down in the air
and curve its parabola
right into your waiting hands.

Pamela Gillilan

10

What You Need to Write a Poem

A piece of meaning.
A peace of time
A peace of patience and some words.
Maybe a picture and some ideas.
And also some time.
You needn't worry about your spelling
Gust rite it down thats all.

Edward★

Words

Inside me
there is a dictionary
with words from my tongue.

Inside me
there is a sentence
I don't understand.

Inside me
there is an invented word
with no meaning.

Inside me
there is a poem
waiting to get out.

Richard★

The Thin Prison

Hold the pen close to your ear.
Listen – can you hear them?
Words burning as a flame,
Words glittering like a tear,

Locked, all locked in the slim pen.
They are crying for freedom.
And you can release them,
Set them running from prison.

Himalayas, balloons, Captain Cook,
Kites, red bricks, London Town,
Sequins, cricket bats, large brown
Boots, lions and lemonade – look,

I've just let them out!
Pick up your pen, and start,
Think of the things you know – then
Let the words dance from your pen.

Leslie Norris

Pen Rhythm

The rhythm of the pen goes bubbling
dancing round the page.
no disease can't cripple it
can't die of old age,
the rhythm of the pen goes to and fro
high and low where you can't go
the rhythm of the pen will not stop now
pen rhythm is in full rage.

The rhythm of the pen goes ring ding dong
left and right and can't go wrong
the pen plans the rhythm and the rhythm sings
the song
the strain is on the rhythm but the rhythm well
strong,
the rhythm of the pen goes here and there
always with harmony always with care
the rhythm is full still there is some spare
pen rhythm get wild pen rhythm don't fear.

Benjamin Zephaniah
(extracts from 'Pen Rhythm')

Poetry Jump-Up

Tell me if ah seeing right
Take a look down de street

Words dancin
words dancin
till dey sweat
words like fishes
jumpin out a net
words wild and free
joinin de poetry revelry
words back to back
words belly to belly

Come on everybody
come and join de poetry band
dis is poetry carnival
dis is poetry bacchanal
when inspiration call
take yu pen in yu hand
if yu dont have a pen
take yu pencil in yu hand
if yu dont have a pencil
what the hell
so long de feeling start to swell
just shout de poem out

Words jumpin off de page
tell me if Ah seein right
words like birds

jumpin out a cage
take a look down de street
words shakin dey waist
words shakin dey bum
words wit black skin
words wit white skin
words wit brown skin
words wit no skin at all
words huggin up words
an sayin I want to be a poem today
rhyme or no rhyme
I is a poem today
I mean to have a good time

Words feelin hot hot hot
big words feelin hot hot hot
lil words feelin hot hot hot
even sad words cant help
tappin dey toe
to de riddum of de poetry band

Dis is poetry carnival
dis is poetry bacchanal
so come on everybody
join de celebration
all yu need is plenty perspiration
an a little inspiration
plenty perspiration
an a little inspiration

John Agard

The Word Party

Loving words clutch crimson roses,
Rude words sniff and pick their noses,
Sly words come dressed up as foxes,
Short words stand on cardboard boxes,
Common words tell jokes and gabble,
Complicated words play Scrabble,
Swear words stamp around and shout,
Hard words stare each other out,
Foreign words look lost and shrug,
Careless words trip on the rug,
Long words slouch with stooping shoulders,
Code words carry secret folders,
Silly words flick rubber bands,
Hyphenated words hold hands,
Strong words show off, bending metal,
Sweet words call each other 'petal',
Small words yawn and suck their thumbs
Till at last the morning comes.
Kind words give out farewell posies . . .

Snap! The dictionary closes.

Richard Edwards

A Song of Myself

There was a naughty boy
    And a naughty boy was he,
For nothing would he do
    But scribble poetry —

He took
An ink stand
In his hand
And a pen
Big as ten
In the other.

And wrote
In his coat
When the weather
Was cool,
Fear of gout,
And without
When the weather
Was warm —

And away
In a Pother
He ran
To the mountains
And fountains
And ghostes
And Postes
And witches
And ditches

Och the charm
When we choose
To follow one's nose
To the north
To the north
To follow one's nose
To the north!

John Keats (1795–1821)

Metaphor

Morning is
a new sheet of paper
for you to write on.

Whatever you want to say,
all day,
until night
folds it up
and files it away.

The bright words and the dark words
are gone
until dawn
and a new day
to write on.

Eve Merriam

Questions

If words
could get up
        and walk away
from the page,
would they
        in their blackness
find a shape?
and you, my dear page
in your emptiness,
would you sing?

G. S. Sharat Chandra

Driving Motor-way Madly

Driving motor-way madly
Through the dictionary
ETCETERA
Striving like an angry bookworm
Starved of print
Is no way
To write a poem.

Let it drop
Like a sycamore seed
Designedly unplanned
To root and grow.
Or drop helpless, but complete
Like calf from cow
Licked, raspingly, into life.

Never write it
While old Super-Eg's awake.
Wait until that bore has nodded off.
Then let out wild and gentle Id
To graze and wander, velvet haltered,
with Ego by his side.

Then pour the poem
On the page
Like pancake batter
In the smoke-hot pan
To choose its own shape,
And grow there
If it can.

Jill Campbell

On the Road Through Chang-te

On the last year's trip I enjoyed this place.
I am glad to come back here today.
The fish market is deep in blue shadows.
I can see the smoke for tea rising
From the thatched inn.
The sands of the river beaches
Merge with the white moon.
Along the shore the willows
Wait for their Spring green.
Lines of a poem run through my mind.
I order the carriage to stop for a while.

Sun Yün-feng (1764–1814)
Translated from the Chinese
by Kenneth Rexroth and Ling Chung

Prose Poem

The days are gold,
and the evenings filled with golden light
as the sun sets.
It is paddy-threshing time,
the great stacks near their heads
like brittle brownhaired men
but the egrets sprinkle a snow-storm.
How beautiful their line of flight,
the positioning of their legs,
and their wings – so
              soft awhite
against the golden sun.
It is winter now – but a winter running away.
The wheat is growing: a sturdy deep-set green
the days are all green and gold
and the birds bring the extra colour –
the jay its blue, the barbets lemon
amidst the green
leaves, which rustle, sing wave hands,
count fingers,
pollenfilled blossoms drift –
and a drift of poems is in the breeze.

Monika Varma

The Poem

It is only a little twig
With a green bud at the end;
But if you plant it,
And water it,
And set it where the sun will be above it,
It will grow into a tall bush
With many flowers,
And leaves which thrust hither and thither
Sparkling.
From its roots will come freshness,
And beneath it the grass-blades
Will bend and recover themselves,
And clash one upon another
In the blowing wind.

But if you take my twig
And throw it into a closet
With mousetraps and blunted tools,
It will shrivel and waste.
And, some day,
When you open the door,
You will think it an old twisted nail,
And sweep it into the dust bin
With other rubbish.

Amy Lowell

Lament

Because I have no time
To set my ladder up, and climb
Out of the dung and straw,
Green poems in a dark store
Shrivel and grow soft
Like unturned apples in a loft.

Jon Stallworthy

Truth

Sticks and stones may break my bones,
but words can also hurt me.
Stones and sticks break only skin,
while words are ghosts that haunt me.

Slant and curved the word-swords fall
to pierce and stick inside me.
Bats and bricks may ache through bones,
but words can mortify me.

Pain from words has left its scar
on mind and heart that's tender.
Cuts and bruises now have healed;
it's words that I remember.

Barrie Wade

Modesties

Words as plain as hen-birds' wings
Do not lie,
Do not over-broider things —
Are too shy.

Thoughts that shuffle round like pence
Through each reign,
Wear down to their simplest sense,
Yet remain.

Weeds are not supposed to grow,
But by degrees
Some achieve a flower, although
No one sees.

Philip Larkin

The Poem Tree

If you see a poem tree
Go to it quick
Pluck a poem
A nice plump fat poem.
Put it carefully in the top
of your pen.
Slowly, gently let it out on the paper.
Change a few words
Let it cool
Then keep it safe.

Josh★

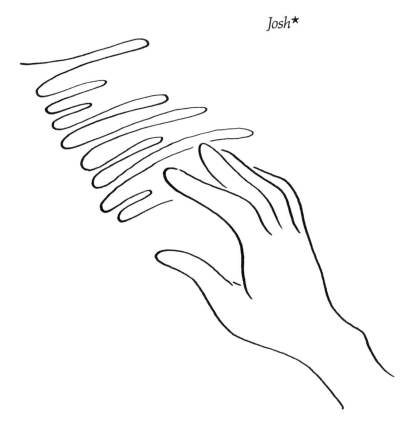

28

Three Birds Flying

Once in a dream
there came to me
three birds flying
one, two, three.

The first was dark as water on a stone,

the second shone bright as sunlight on a stone,

and the third was gray as a stone, as a stone.

I rode with them
as they flew on,
but when I woke
the dream was gone.

I set it down on paper
and the words are there;
and every time I read it,
the birds are there.

Eve Merriam

29

Halfway

I saw a tadpole once in a sheet of ice
(a freakish joke played by my country's weather).
He hung at arrest, displayed as it were in glass,
an illustration of neither one thing nor the other.

His head was a frog's and his hinder legs had grown
ready to climb and jump to his promised land;
but his bladed tail in the ice-pane weighed him down.
He seemed to accost my eye with his budding hand.

'I am neither one thing nor the other, not here
                              nor there.
I saw great lights in the place where I would be,
but rose too soon, half made for water, half air,
and they have gripped and stilled and enchanted me.'

'Is that world real, or a dream I cannot reach?
Beneath me the dark familiar waters flow
and my fellows huddle and nuzzle each to each,
while motionless here I stare where I cannot go.'

The comic O of his mouth, his gold-rimmed eyes,
looked in that lustrous glaze as though they'd ask
my vague divinity, looming in stooped surprise,
for death or rescue. But neither was my task.

Waking halfway from a dream one winter night
I remembered him as a poem I had to write.

Judith Wright

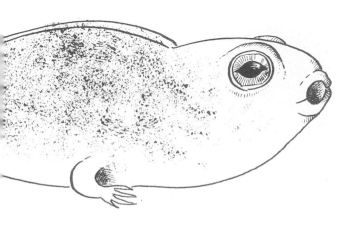

The Thought-Fox

I imagine this midnight moment's forest:
Something else is alive
Beside the clock's loneliness
And this blank page where my fingers move.

Through the window I see no star:
Something more near
Though deeper within darkness
Is entering the loneliness:

Cold, delicately as the dark snow
A fox's nose touches twig, leaf;
Two eyes serve a movement, that now
And again now, and now, and now

Sets neat prints into the snow
Between trees, and warily a lame
Shadow lags by stump and in hollow
Of a body that is bold to come

Across clearings, an eye,
A widening deepening greenness,
Brilliantly, concentratedly,
Coming about its own business

Till, with a sudden sharp hot stink of fox
It enters the dark hole of the head.
The window is starless still; the clock ticks,
The page is printed.

Ted Hughes

What the Chairman Told Tom

POETRY? It's a hobby.
I run model trains.
Mr Shaw there breeds pigeons.

It's not work. You don't sweat.
Nobody pays for it.
You *could* advertise soap.

Art, that's opera; or repertory —
The Desert Song.
Nancy was in the chorus.

But to ask for twelve pounds a week —
married, aren't you? —
you've got a nerve.

How could I look a bus conductor
in the face
if I paid you twelve pounds?

Who says it's poetry, anyhow?
My ten year old
can do it *and* rhyme.

I get three thousand and expenses
a car, vouchers,
but I'm an accountant.

They do what I tell them,
my company.
What do *you* do?

Nasty little words, nasty long words,
it's unhealthy.
I want to wash when I meet a poet.

They're Reds, addicts,
all delinquents.
What they write is rot.

Mr Hines says so, and he's a schoolteacher,
he ought to know.
Go and find *work*.

Basil Bunting

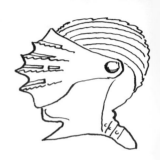

A Good Poem

I like a good poem
one with lots of fighting
in it. Blood and the
clanging of armour. Poems

against Scotland are good
and poems that defeat
the French with crossbows.
I don't like poems that

aren't about anything.
Sonnets are wet and
a waste of time.
Also poems that don't

know how to rhyme.
If I was a poem
I'd play football and
get picked for England.

Roger McGough

An Attempt at Unrhymed Verse

People tell you all the time,
Poems do not have to rhyme.
It's often better if they don't
And I'm determined this one won't.
                              Oh dear.

Never mind, I'll start again.
Busy, busy with my pen ... cil.
I can do it if I try –
Easy, peasy, pudding and gherkins.

Writing verse is so much fun,
Cheering as the summer weather,
Makes you feel alert and bright,
'Specially when you get it more or less the
                              way you want it.

Wendy Cope

Word

The word bites like a fish
Shall I throw it back free
Arrowing to that sea
Where thoughts lash tail and fin?
Or shall I pull it in
To rhyme upon a dish?

Stephen Spender

W

The King sent for his wise men all
To find a rhyme for W;
When they had thought a good long time
But could not think of a single rhyme,
'I'm sorry,' said he, 'to trouble you.'

James Reeves

The Aesthetic Weasel

A weasel
perched on an easel
within a patch of teasel.

But why
and how?

The Moon Cow
whispered her reply
one time:

The sopheest-
icated beest
just did it for the rhyme.

Christian Morgenstern

Rhymes

Two respectable rhymes
skipped out of their pages
like two proud roosters
from golden cages;

they walked many a mile
in search of a home,
but could find no space
for themselves in a poem.

They grew tired and sad
but wherever they went
nobody advertised
poems for rent.

People whispered and said:
haven't you heard
that a rhyming word
is considered absurd?

In modern times
who needs rhymes?
Those high-flying words
went out with the birds.

At last one night
all weary and worn
they came to a house
in a field of corn;

and there lived a man
who still wrote lines
according to rules
from olden times.

So he took them in
with doubles and pairs,
and set them to music,
and gave them new airs.

Now they ring again
their bells and chimes,
and the children all sing
those respectable rhymes,

with one rhyme inside
and another one out:
the rhymes were befriended
and my poem is ended.

Y. Y. Segal
Translated from the Yiddish
by Miriam Waddington

Haiku

hai-ku

      hai-ku

            hai-

coo the pigeons

in springtime

      -ku

        hai-ku

            hai-ku.

Adrian Henri

First Haiku of Spring

	cuck	oo	cuck	oo	cuck	
oo	cuck	oo	cuck	oo	cuck	oo
	cuck	oo	cuck	oo	cuck	

Roger McGough

On Basho's Frog

Under the cloudy cliff, near the temple door,
Between dusky spring plants on the pond,
A frog jumps in the water, plop!
Startled, the poet drops his brush.

Sengai (18th Century)
Translated from the Japanese
by Lucien Stryk

The poet Saigyō
Would have written a poem
Even for the woman
Washing potatoes.

Matsuo Basho (18th Century)
Translated from the Japanese
by Nobuyuki Yuasa

The Flea

I think that I shall never see
A poem livelier than a Flea.

Frank Collymore

Well, it's partly the shape of the thing
That makes the old limerick swing —
Its accordion pleats
Full of light, airy beats
Take it up like a kite on the wing!

Anonymous

London Airport

Last night in London Airport
I saw a wooden bin
labelled UNWANTED LITERATURE
IS TO BE PLACED HEREIN.
So I wrote a poem
and popped it in.

Christopher Logue

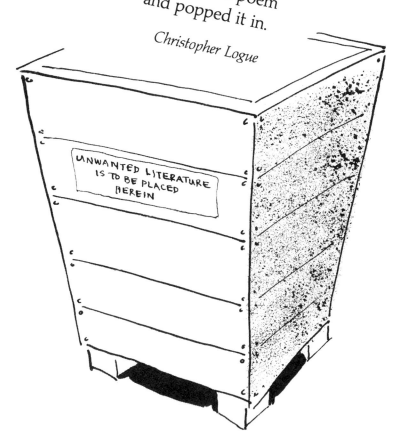

UNWANTED LITERATURE
IS TO BE PLACED
HEREIN

The Dis-satisfied Poem

I'm a dissatisfied poem
    I really am
there's so many things
    I don't understand
like why I'm lying
    on this flat white page
when there's so much to do
    in the world out there
But sometimes when I catch a glimpse
    of the world outside
it makes my blood curl
    it makes me want to stay inside
and hide
    please turn me quick
before I cry
    they would hate it if I wet the pages

Grace Nichols

What is Poetry?

Look at those naked words dancing together!
Everyone's very embarrassed.
Only one thing to do about it –
Off with your clothes
And join in the dance.
Naked words and people dancing together.
There's going to be trouble.
Here come the Poetry Police!

Keep dancing.

Adrian Mitchell
(extract from 'What is Poetry?')

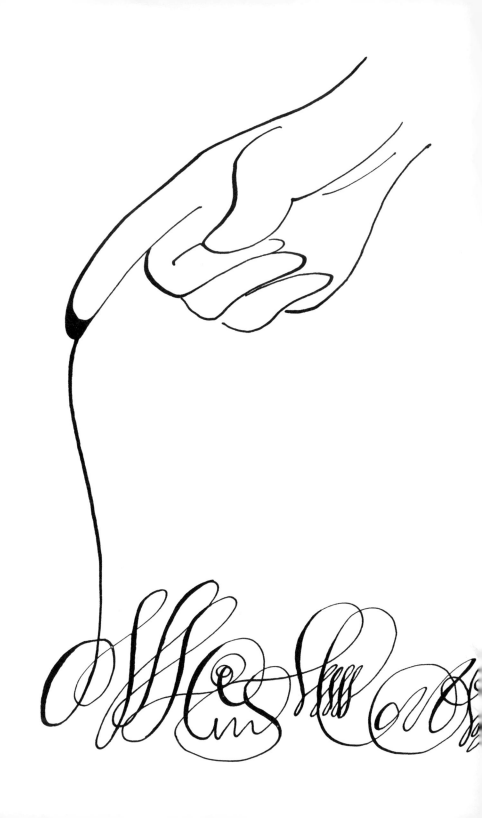

Poem on Bread

The poet is about to write a poem:
He does not use a pencil or a pen.
He dips his long thin finger into jam
Or something savoury preferred by men.
This poet does not choose to write on paper;
He takes a single slice of well-baked bread
And with his jam or marmite-nibbed forefinger
He writes his verses down on that instead.
His poem is fairly short as all the best are.
When he has finished it he hopes that you
Or someone else – your brother, friend or sister –
Will read and find it marvellous and true.
If you can't read, then eat: it tastes quite good.
If you do neither, all that I can say
Is he who needs no poetry or bread
Is really in a devilish bad way.

Vernon Scannell

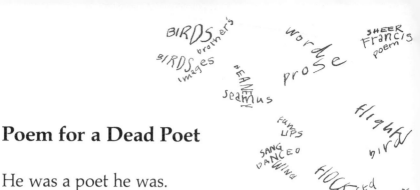

Poem for a Dead Poet

He was a poet he was.
A proper poet.
He said things
that made you think
and said them nicely.
He saw things
that you or I
could never see
and saw them clearly.
He had a way
with language.
Images flocked around
him like birds,
St Francis, he was,
of the words. Words?
Why he could almost make 'em talk.

Roger McGough

Saint Francis and the Birds

When Francis preached love to the birds
They listened, fluttered, throttled up
Into the blue like a flock of words

Released for fun from his holy lips.
Then wheeled back, whirred about his head,
Pirouetted on brother's capes,

Danced on the wing, for sheer joy played
And sang, like images took flight.
Which was the best poem Francis made,

His argument true, his tone light.

Seamus Heaney

Dreamcut

I will make poems like people

like animals walking through light
like birds more slender than a spear
like swords with faces and delicate feet
like dreams carved black in the head's cave
like hair, shag, dread
silence will never diminish

because that is how we come bright
to each other, shaking
the wet from us like fishernets,
that is how the skin
catches air
and the heavy faces
flung into rainbow haloes
and old, old, old.

Dennis Scott

The Poet Says Goodbye to his Friends

Brothers, give me quickly
A feather-pen to write with,
A paper clean and shining
To fill up full with rhymes,
With good ink from the cuttle fish
To write it bright and readable,
And you – you keep your eyes awake,
And as you go, take care!

Ahmad Nassir

The Pool

Ripples from a stone
     Dropped in a pool
Like a poem's meaning
     Go travelling on

Ruth Dallas

Once Upon a Time

Once upon a time there lived
a small joke
in the middle of nowhere.

This small joke
was dying to share
itself with someone

but nobody came to hear
this small joke.

So this small joke told
itself to the birds

and the birds told this small joke to the trees
and the trees told this small joke to the rivers
and the rivers told this small joke to the mountains
and the mountains told this small joke to the stars

till the whole world
started to swell with laughter

and nobody believed
it all began
with a small joke

that lived in the middle of nowhere.

Everybody kept saying

it was me
it was me.

John Agard

Forgotten Language

Once I spoke the language of the flowers,
Once I understood each word the caterpillar said,
Once I smiled in secret at the gossip of the starlings,
And shared a conversation with the housefly
            in my bed.
Once I heard and answered all the questions
            of the crickets,
And joined the crying of each falling dying
            flake of snow,
Once I spoke the language of the flowers ...
            How did it go?
            How did it go?

Shel Silverstein

Orders

Muffle the wind;
Silence the clock;
Muzzle the mice;
Curb the small talk;
Cure the hinge — squeak;
Banish the thunder,
Let me sit silent,
Let me wonder.

A. M. Klein

I am the Song

I am the song that sings the bird.
I am the leaf that grows the land.
I am the tide that moves the moon.
I am the stream that halts the sand.
I am the cloud that drives the storm.
I am the earth that lights the sun.
I am the fire that strikes the stone.
I am the clay that shapes the hand.
I am the word that speaks the man.

Charles Causley

'And what,' said the Emperor, 'does this poem describe?'
'It describes,' said the Poet, 'the cave of the Never-Never,
Would you like to see what's inside?' He offered his arm.
They stepped into the poem and disappeared forever.

George Barker

Index of titles

First lines are given for those poems without titles
An asterisk indicates a poem written by a young person

60

Acknowledgements

We are grateful to the following for permission to reproduce copyright material: **John Agard** courtesy of Caroline Sheldon Literary Agency for 'Once Upon a Time' from *Laughter is an Egg*, Viking Kestrel, 1990. © John Agard; 'Poetry Jump-up' from *You'll Love this Stuff*, Cambridge University Press, 1987. © John Agard. **George Barker** for "'And what,' said the Emperor, 'does this poem describe?'" **Jill Campbell** for 'Driving Motor-way Madly'. **Laura Cecil** for 'W' by James Reeves from *The Wandering Moon and Other Poems* by James Reeves. Reprinted by permission of the James Reeves Estate. © James Reeves. **Frank Collymore** for 'The Flea' from the *Talk of the Tamarinds*, edited by A. Forde, 1972. **Wendy Cope** for 'An Attempt at Unrhymed Verse'. **Curtis Brown** for 'The Dis-Satisfied Poem' by Grace Nichols from *There's a Poet Behind You*, A & C Black, 1988. © Grace Nichols 1988. **Ruth Dallas and Otago University Press** for 'The Pool' from *Songs for a Guitar*, edited by C. Brash, 1976. **Richard Edwards** for 'The Word Party' from *The Word Party*, 1986. **Faber & Faber** for 'Modesties' by Philip Larkin from *The Collected Poems of Philip Larkin*; 'Saint Francis and the Birds' by Seamus Heaney from *Death of a Naturalist*; 'The Thought-Fox' from *Hawk in the Rain* by Ted Hughes, 1957; 'Word' by Stephen Spender from *Collected Poems 1928–1985*. **Pamela Gillilan** for 'Poetry (or Cricket)' from *A Fifth Poetry Book*, edited by John Foster, Oxford University Press, 1985. **Adrian Henri** for 'Haiku' from *The Phantom Lollipop Lady*, Methuen, 1986. **Roger McGough** for 'A Good Poem' from *In the Glassroom*, Jonathan Cape; 'Poem for a Dead Poet' from *Holiday on Death Row*, Jonathan Cape. **London Magazine Editions** for 'Questions' by G. S. Sharat Chandra from *April in Nanjangud*, 1971. **Gerda Mayer** for 'Shallow Poem' from *The Knockabout Show*, Chatto & Windus, 1978. **Methuen Childrens Books** for an extract from *The House at Pooh Corner*, by A. A. Milne. **Leslie Norris** for 'The Thin Prison' from *Drumming in the Sky*, edited by Paddy Bachely, BBC Publications. **Oxford University Press** for 'Lament' by Jon Stallworthy from *The Astronomy of Love*, 1961; 'Truth' by Barrie Wade from *Conkers*, 1989. © Barrie Wade 1989; 'What the Chairman Told Tom' from *The Collected Poems of Basil Bunting*, 1978. © Basil Bunting 1978. **Penguin Books** for an extract from 'The Poet Saigyō' from *The Narrow Road to the Deep North and Other Travel Sketches* translated by Nobuyuki Yuasa (Penguin Classics, 1966) translation © Nobuyuki Yuasa, 1966. **Peter Fraser & Dunlop** for 'First Haiku of Spring' by Roger McGough from *Nailing the Shadow*, Viking Kestrel, 1987; An extract from 'What is Poetry?' by Adrian Mitchell from *On the Beach at Cambridge*, Allison & Busby Limited, 1984: neither this work nor any other is to be used in connection with any examination whatsoever. **Marian Reiner** for 'Metaphor' and 'Three Birds Flying' by Eve Merriam from *A Sky Full of Poems*. © 1964, 1970, 1973 Eve Merriam. **K. Rexroth & Ling Chung** for 'On the Road Through Chang-te' by Sun Yün-feng from *The Orchid Boat: Women Poets of China*, translated and edited by K. Rexroth & Ling Chung. **Vernon Scannell** for 'Poem on Bread'. **Dennis Scott** for 'Dreamcul' from *Dreadwalk*, 1982. **Shel Silverstein** for 'Forgotten Language' from *Where the Sidewalk Ends*, Jonathan Cape, 1978. **Lucien Stryk** for 'On Basho's Frog' by Sengai from the *Penguin Book of Zen Poetry*. **Turret Books** for 'London Airport' by Christopher Logue from *Ode to the Dodo Poems*, 1953–1978. **University of California** for 'The Aesthetic Weasel' by Christian Morgenstern from *The Gallows Songs*, translated & edited by Knight & Max. © 1963 Knight & Max. **University of Toronto Press** for 'Orders' by A. M. Klein from *Complete Poetry Volume One*, A. M. Klein, edited by Zailing Pollock. © University of Toronto Press, 1990. **University of Wisconsin Press** for 'The Poet says Goodbye to his Friends' by Ahmad Nassir from *Poems from Kenya: Gnomic Verses in Swahili* by Ahmad Nassir Bin Juma Bhalo, translated by Lyndon Harries © 1966. **Monika Varma** for 'Prose Poem' from *Greenleaves and Gold*, Writers' Workshop, Calcutta, 1970. **Miriam Waddington** for the translation of Y. Y. Segal's poem 'Rhymes' from *The New Wind Has Wings*, Oxford University Press, Canada. **Clive Wake & Dennis Reed** for the translation of Malick Fall's poem 'Empty Head' from *French African Verse*, Heinemann, 1972. **Judith Wright** for 'Halfway'. **Benjamin Zephaniah** for 'Pen Rhythm' from *The Dread Affair*, Random Century Limited.

Every effort has been made to trace and acknowledge copyright, but in some cases copyright proved untraceable. If any right has been omitted, the publishers offer their apologies and will rectify this in subsequent editions following notification.